Ted and Trapper Joe

JUNIOR BOOKS

DOUBLEDAY & COMPANY, INC

GARDEN CITY NEW YORK

BOOKS BY

SANFORD TOUSEY

COWBOY TOMMY

COWBOY TOMMY'S ROUNDUP

JERRY AND THE PONY EXPRESS

VAL RIDES THE OREGON TRAIL

STAGECOACH SAM

BOB AND THE RAILROAD

AIRPLANE ANDY

DICK AND THE CANAL BOAT

FRED AND BROWN BEAVER RIDE THE RIVER

TED AND TRAPPER JOE

 Lithographed in the United States of America by Michaelson Lithograph Corporation.

TED and his twin brother, Harry, were traveling across the plains in a big covered wagon. For weeks their father, Mort Downs, had driven his team of horses along the Western trail. He was taking his family to a "promised land" where crops would grow in abundance.

"It may be *Oregon* an' it may be *Californy*," he told his faithful, uncomplaining wife. "We'll decide when we get to Fort Bridger."

The horses were unhitched, hobbled, and allowed to graze. Mrs. Downs handed each boy his bowl of gruel and some stewed dried apples. She did her cooking over an open campfire. His supper over, Ted climbed up into the covered wagon and lay down on his blanket. Harry went out to the horses.

Suddenly Ted heard a shout from his father. Peering over the wagon seat, he saw feathered horsemen galloping toward them.

His mother quickly climbed into the wagon. "Get the rifles, Mary!" yelled Mr. Downs as he ran toward them. "It's Indians!"

Ted saw Harry reach for the lead ropes of Nick and Zeb, the horses, to bring them in. At that moment a painted Indian galloped up to Harry. Grabbing Harry's collar, he lifted the boy before him onto his pony and sped away.

Mort Downs was a good rifle shot. His first two bullets hit galloping redskins. As fast as he fired, Mrs. Downs reloaded the muzzle-loading rifles. The Indians were circling round and round the wagon now. Many of their arrows were coming through the canvas sides.

"Come here, Ted," said his father as he lifted the top of the wagon seat and shoved the boy under it.

Ted lay quietly on a blanket in the darkness of the seat box. He could hear the "plunk, plunk" of Indian arrows as they struck the side of the wagon. This was followed by two shots from his father's rifle. Then they were silent. Peeking through a crack, Ted saw his father slumped down with an arrow through his middle. Then the rifles spoke again as Mary Downs loaded them and fired. The yells of the Indians became louder as they circled closer. Soon Mary's rifles were silenced. Then Ted knew that both his parents were gone.

He lay as still as a mouse while the savages ransacked the wagon and made off with their booty and scalps. It was a long time after the Indians left before Ted managed to get the seat top up and looked around. Harry and the horses were gone. Tears flowed down Ted's cheeks as he saw what the Indians had done to his parents.

He didn't know what to do, so when darkness came he rolled up in his blanket. But it was hours before he fell into a restless sleep.

Ted was aroused at dawn by the sound of horses' hoofs. He looked out over the tailboard at the queerest figure he had ever seen. It was a bewhiskered man dressed in a fringed buckskin suit. He rode a horse and led a pack horse and a pack mule. On his head was a coonskin cap. He held his muzzle-loading rifle across the saddle in front of him. His powder horn and bullet pouch hung from buckskin straps thrown over his shoulder. His bag of "possibles" hung from his belt. So did several scalps taken from Indians he had killed.

When he saw the covered wagon with arrows sticking in it he stopped his animals and murmured, "Injuns got 'em!"

Then he spied Ted's head peering over the tailboard.

"Well, sonny," he said, "you holdin' the fort all alone?"

Ted was so glad to hear his friendly voice that words began pouring from him. He told the man all that had happened the day before.

"I'm Joe Bouton," the man told Ted. "I'm one of the Mountain Men that traps furs in these parts. You'd better come along with me. Mebbe we'll meet up with some other wagon that ye can join. But first get me that shovel off the mule's back. We'll give yer folks a decent burial."

This they did. Then, at Joe's direction, Ted clambered onto the back of the pack horse. As they rode off Ted turned for a last sad look at the deserted wagon.

"Keep a stiff upper lip, Bud," cautioned Ted's new friend. "Life on the plains is onsartin. Here today and gone tomorrow."

Ted noticed that Joe's keen eyes were continually glancing to the left and right. Occasionally he gave a backward glance.

"Lookin' fer Injun sign," said the trapper to Ted. "You must learn to keep yer eyes open. If ye don't, yer a gone goose.

"I don't think the Injuns will be back," he continued. "They took everything worth taking. Here's where we turn off."

They had been following the main westward wagon trail. Now Joe turned south, down through a deep, pleasant gully. A hundred yards farther he called a halt.

"Tie yer horse and come with me," the trapper said as he returned to the main trail. There he got down on hands and knees and rapidly covered the horses' hoofprints with dry dust. This he did for the full hundred yards back to their animals. Not a sign of their entrance was left at the gully's opening.

For the next two days Ted followed Joe's lead along the old buffalo trail that they were taking to Joe's hunting ground. Toward noon of the second day Joe sniffed the air with uplifted nose.

"Smoke!" he exclaimed, halting his horse. "It's Injuns, probably. Tie the horses and we'll climb up to that point and take a look at the land."

It was a stiff climb, and Ted was out of breath when Joe held up his hand to halt. He pointed down a valley that paralleled theirs. Ted gazed at the first Indian village he had ever seen. Tepees were set along the banks of a stream. Smoke floated up from the vents in their tops. Squaws were busy drying meat on racks. Children and dogs ran about the tepees. A band of hunters on their ponies was just arriving home with fresh meat.

"Take a good look, Ted, an' let's get goin'," said Joe. "Wind might change an' blow our scent down to their dogs. Then we'd be in for it!"

Joe ordered a wide detour from the valley they were in.

That meant another steep climb to the eastward.

"But it's over hard rock, an' we'll leave no trail for their scouts to find," Joe assured Ted.

They made the wide semicircle around the Indian camp and got back to the buffalo trail. Four more days of travel brought them to the place Joe was looking for.

Ted had never seen such a beautiful spot. It was a valley with rocky hills on each side. Long green grass, spotted with wild flowers, formed the floor. Down the center flowed a silver stream from which trout splashed. Willows and cottonwoods lined its banks. Farther up on the hillside evergreens grew plentifully.

"Don't this suit us!" exclaimed Joe. "Now, Bud, before we set up camp let's look fer Indian sign. You take the sunny side of the valley and I'll take the shady side. Keep yer eyes open, Ted, an' remember all I've taught ye this past week."

Ted felt happy to know that Joe trusted him. If he made a mistake and failed to see any Indian sign that might be there, it could easily mean the end of them.

Back and forth he rode, searching the ground carefully, but not a sign could he find. Joe reported the same as they both rode into the camp site.

"Now for a wickiup," ordered Joe. "Get your ax. We'll build it deep in this clump of bushes and hide it under 'em so well that no Injun will stumble onto it."

Joe stretched his ridgepole between the crotches of two saplings. Against the ridgepole he leaned the saplings that formed the roof. On this they placed squares of tough sod to shed rain.

By the time they had finished their shelter they were

both ready to eat. Joe caught two trout from the creek. Ted built the fire, Indian fashion, with the sticks pointing toward the center and small stones encircling it. Joe had taught Ted to do this.

"When Injuns find a white man's fire they start looking for him," Joe had told him. "Might just as well build an Injun fire an' mebbe save yer scalp."

That night they slept under a roof for the first time in days. Ted carried pine needles inside to make their beds. On these they spread their blankets.

Before Joe went to sleep he remarked, "Plenty of beaver signs in the creek. You're a lucky mascot, Ted."

Joe awakened Ted at daylight next morning. "We've a big day ahead, setting our traps," said Joe. He took Ted along and showed him how to cut the stakes and place them well out in the stream. To these the traps were fastened by chains. Sometimes Joe used a wooden float.

Ted soon learned all the tricks of trapping and attended to his half of the traps. Joe trained him well in handling the pelts. Their pile of beaver furs grew and grew. One morning Joe said, "Tain't good to have all our eggs in one basket. Thieving Injuns could make off with the whole lot. We'll divide 'em into four lots an' hide 'em."

So they made four hiding places at a distance and placed their beaver skins, or "plew," as Joe called them, inside. They carefully covered all telltale marks.

"Injuns will never find 'em," Joe assured Ted. But Joe did not know that even then a couple of redskin hunters had been spying on them from the distant evergreens. The Indians had marked the hiding places. Next day, when Joe and Ted returned from their traps, they found that three of their four stores had been robbed.

"The rapscallions!" shouted Joe when he discovered their loss. He jumped on his horse and galloped in the direction taken by the thieves. But when he cooled off he realized the robbers had had many hours' start and that his horse was not fresh.

He dismounted and examined the tracks left by the Indians. "Just a couple of 'em," he murmured to himself. "Probably young braves foraging far from their tribe an' lookin' fer excitement."

Joe turned back to camp, where he told Ted the news.

"All we can do is to start in again," he said. "Lucky fer us, beaver is plentiful. Mebbe by spring we can make up fer it."

So they worked harder than ever. This time they made new hiding places. In the dark of night they carried their furs inside these. Then they covered their tracks.

As the weather had become colder they had added to their hut. Then they completely enclosed it. In the center of the roof they left a hole big enough to carry out the smoke from their fire.

Ted had been a good shot with his father's rifle. Now Joe sometimes let him use his rifle. Ted brought in squirrels and wild fowl to be cooked over their campfire. Joe could be depended upon to supply deermeat and larger game. They had plenty to eat. Most of it was meat from wild animals. Joe showed Ted how to make hoecake from cornmeal and water, baked at the fireplace.

Joe used the skin from a deer's leg to carry water up from the creek. He had removed the skin nearly whole from the leg of the deer. The larger upper opening he sewed together. In the lower small opening he placed a plug that could be pulled out to release the water. It was a trick Joe had learned from the Indians, and it worked very well.

Ted returned to camp one evening with some extra-fine pelts. He was anxious to show them to Joe and hear his praises. But Joe did not show up. Darkness came on, but no sign of Joe. Ted was worried. Making sure his hunting knife was in his belt, Ted picked up an ax and started for Joe's trapping ground. The moon had come up brightly, and Ted followed Joe's path. Every few minutes he stopped and listened intently. Finally, through the stillness, he heard

a faint moan. Hurrying his pace, he came upon Joe, half submerged in the cold water of the creek. A tree across his leg was pinning him down.

"The durned beavers turned the tables an' trapped *me!*" said Joe faintly. "They chawed that tree nearly in two to make their dam. I didn't notice it was cut. While I was settin' my trap it fell on my leg. Lucky you were near, Bud, or I'd a been a gone goose."

Ted fell to with his ax. He had used the ax aplenty that winter, and it did not take him long to free Joe's leg. Then he helped the Mountain Man to a dry spot on the creek bank. Once out of the cold water, Joe's leg began to swell. Ted cut open Joe's buckskin leggings with his knife. Joe took a look at the black-and-blue swelling.

"Go bring my horse, Ted. My rifle is against that tree. Better hand it to me in case a grizzly b'ar gets curious while you're gone," ordered Joe.

As quickly as he could Ted returned with Joe's horse Baldy, all saddled. Joe hopped on one leg over to a stump while Ted held Baldy. Joe used his rifle as a support and managed to scramble onto the horse's back for the ride home. At camp Ted made Joe comfortable on his blanket in their hut. Then Ted bound Joe's swollen leg.

"I can still do a little cookin'," said the Mountain Man. "But, Ted, you'll have to mind all the traps as best ye can. I'm laid up fer a week at least."

But in less than a week the wiry Mountain Man was hobbling around to his traps with the aid of a cane he had cut. Ted was glad for his help. The extra work at the traps had doubled Ted's labor, and he was fagged out. Before long Joe lost all trace of his limp.

Early one morning they were awakened by noises down at the creek. Joe grabbed his rifle while Ted cautiously peeked out of the door.

"It's a pair of strange horses," said Ted. "They look like Nick and Zeb, our team. They must have broken away from the Indians' herd."

"Don't scare 'em away, Bud!" whispered Joe. "Creep up on 'em, gentle like. We need 'em bad to help carry all them furs out o' here. It's a godsend if we catch 'em."

Ted crept out ever so slowly, giving the low whistle he had often heard his father use when bridling the horses. Nick was the gentler member of the team. When he heard the whistle and smelled Ted's scent, he walked toward Ted and was soon tied. Zeb had other ideas. He had been living a free life for weeks. This was no time to be put to work!

"I'll saddle my horse and rope Zeb!" exclaimed Joe as he started for the place they kept the horses and mule. Zeb ran to the edge of their clearing and acted skittish. But Joe was an old hand with horses. He rode in from a rear path and had his rope around Zeb's neck before Zeb could bolt.

"Two good horses, an' they both look sound an' well fed. Must of found good grazing. When we get some of those cockleburs out of their manes an' tails an' rub off the mud they've rolled in, they'll be good as new! Now we can make packsaddles fer 'em an' get our beaver to the Rendezvous." Joe was happy at having one of his problems solved.

He had explained to Ted that the Rendezvous was a yearly meeting of Mountain Men, Indians, trappers, and traders. They brought in their season's catch of furs. Fur buyers from farther east came with their trade goods and whisky. It was an exciting time for Indians and white men. There were lively celebrations and many fights.

Joe showed Ted how to make a packsaddle. In a short time they had two of them ready for Nick and Zeb.

"Time to git a-goin'!" said Joe. "Tomorrow we'll pack our beaver on the hosses and break camp. We'll git to the Rendezvous early and trade in our pelts."

Ted helped Joe pack the horses early next morning. Their hut had become a pleasant home to both of them. It was hard to leave the little valley with its silver stream.

"Never mind, Bud," Joe assured Ted. "We'll come back again. This is too good to leave forever."

They made good time the first day. That night they sat beside their campfire and rested. Joe watched Ted throwing his hunting knife so that it would stick in a tree.

"Not that way, Ted," he cautioned. "Hold yer knife like this. Then throw it so's it will turn over several times before it hits the tree. Plenty of practice will show ye jist how many times to make the knife turn in the air before it strikes. Mountain Men seldom miss at knife throwin'." Now that the furs were packed Joe had more time to teach Ted.

Ted was determined to be a good knife thrower. He practiced every evening. At last Joe said, "Now yer gettin' somewhere, Ted. You'll be a Mountain Man yet!"

After more than a week on the trail Ted watched Joe sniff the air one warm afternoon.

"I smell smoke!" exclaimed Joe. "We must be nearing the Rendezvous. Look! Just over that hill. Smoke from many fires! Here we are, Ted. Our troubles are over. Now for a big celebration!"

And a big celebration it proved to be! Ted had never imagined anything like it.

As they approached the Rendezvous, Ted could see the big log building that had been raised by the men as a trading post and fort. It was in a sharp bend in the creek. To the west was the Indian camp with many tepees. To the east were the campfires, blankets, and equipment of the Mountain Men and trappers—dozens of them.

Joe led the way along a path that took them to the trappers' campground. No sooner did Joe and Ted appear than three whiskered Mountain Men arose with loud shouts. They set down their cups near their keg of whisky and ran toward Joe. Good-naturedly, they slapped and pounded his back until he lost his breath. Then two of them lifted him on their shoulders and carried him to the group of trappers at their camp.

"Here's old Trapper Joe Bouton!" they shouted. "And look at the plew he's bringing in. Where'd ye find all that beaver, Joe?"

One trapper spied Ted looking on in wonderment. "Is that your cub, Joe?" he asked. "Did ye find him in the mountains?"

Joe sobered at once. "He's a good kid an' 'good medicine,'" he replied. "I found him in a covered wagon over

toward the Sweetwater. Pawnees killed his parents an' run off with his twin brother. He's been doin' a man's work helpin' me trap all season. When a log pinned me down like a trapped beaver, he got me out while I still had breath left in me. An' he's learned to throw his knife like a true Mountain Man!"

A few grunts of "Ugh!" came from several trappers, and Ted could tell from their faces that they were impressed by Joe's praise of him. It took unusual deeds to win the praise of an old-timer like Joe.

"I'll be back as soon as I unload," Joe told the men.

"Come on, Ted," he continued. "We'll take our beaver over to the post."

Trading had already begun at the post. Once there, Joe showed the fur buyer the fine quality of the pelts he and Ted had brought in. There was much talk back and forth before they were purchased and added to the huge piles in the store.

Then Joe was handed his gold coins, which he placed in the pouch at his belt. Before leaving, Joe purchased things he needed to replenish his stock: bullets, powder, caps, food, and "possibles" for his pouch.

"Our new moccasins and leggin's we'll get from squaws over at the Indian camp. They're cheap an' good," announced Joe.

Ted's eyes were attracted by the new rifles suspended on pegs in the wall. Joe saw the longing look on the boy's face.

"Want one o' them, Bud?" Joe asked. "Nobody that kin shoot as well as you should be without a rifle! Hand me down the best one thar!" he called to the clerk.

Joe held it to his shoulder to sight along the barrel and get the feel of it.

"Seems like a good one to me," he remarked. "Has all the latest trimmin's. Course I wouldn't trade my old 'Mary Ann' fer it. There never was a rifle as good as my 'Mary Ann.'"

But Ted was too happy to argue. Now he had a rifle all his own to do as he pleased with!

Joe bought Ted a pouch and the bullets to go into it, powder, and caps.

"There're plenty o' buffalo horns around. You can whittle one down tonight in camp. That will carry yer powder," said Joe. "You've earned this, Ted." It took one of Joe's biggest gold coins to settle the bill, but he paid cheerfully.

"Now we'll go to the Injun's camp fer our moccasins. That's why I bought this jewelry and vermilion here. The squaws are anxious to trade fer it."

They crossed over to the spot on the creek bank where the Indian village was encamped.

"Look like Crow Injuns to me," remarked Joe. "Their squaws are handy with their needles."

Ted was interested in the bright colored pictures that the Indians had painted on the outside of their tepees. They liked to picture the shining sun, birds, buffaloes, and horses.

As they approached the village Joe held his jewelry on high. The squaws knew what this meant, and soon a dozen Indian women surrounded them. Joe knew enough Indian words to be able to tell them, with the aid of the sign language, what he needed. When the trading was over, Ted had two pairs of moccasins, new buckskin leggings, and a buckskin jacket, all trimmed with fringe and colored beads. Joe had an outfit just like it.

One of the squaws had been looking hard at Ted. Then she called another squaw and pointed at Ted's hair and face. They chattered at one another. Ted began to wonder what it was all about. They talked too fast for Joe to understand.

Then one of the squaws gave an order to a young Indian boy. He scampered off to the far end of the village. Ted spied him a few minutes later. He was leading a white boy about Ted's size.

When the two boys saw each other they could hardly believe their eyes. For the white boy from the Indian camp was Ted's twin brother, Harry.

"I thought you were dead, Harry!" exclaimed Ted.

"And that's just what I thought of you!" replied Harry. "You see, after that band of Pawnee warriors carried me off, they got into a battle with these Crows. The Crows took me away from the Pawnees and made me a member of their tribe.

The Crows have treated me well. I like them. And I like being an Indian! The Crows shot many of the Pawnees who killed our parents."

Then Ted told his brother how Joe Bouton had taught him the ways of the Mountain Men. He showed Harry his new rifle and clothes and explained how kind Joe had been to him.

Harry led Ted to the tepee he now called home. He pointed out his regular spot inside and where each member of the family sat. Ted noticed how the fire in the center was all ringed around with stones. Indian children peeked in at them as the brothers talked. Every day after that the two met, either at the Indian tepee or at Joe's camp.

Each night Joe left Ted in charge of their camp while he went visiting the camps of the other trappers. Many of these had gambled or spent all of their earnings. Now they had to borrow from a fur trader in order to live until next season's furs were marketed. They were a happy, careless lot. Many narrow escapes had taught them not to worry about anything. When food was scarce they could always kill a buffalo or some game.

The end of the Rendezvous was approaching. Joe spoke to Ted. "Bud," he said, "you've enjoyed trappin' with me. But you're only a youngster and have many years ahead of you. That goes fer yer brother, too. Harry seems to have 'gone Indian.' But both of ye should be with yer folks back East, away from this killin' an' danger. Bring him over here. I want to talk to both of ye."

So Ted went after Harry. When they were all seated around the campfire, Joe repeated what he had said to Ted. Harry objected to leaving his Indian home and foster parents. They had allowed him the freedom that all Indian boys had around their camp. He was a "blood brother" of the Indians now, and if he deserted them they would be enraged. They might even pursue him and Ted and severely punish both of them.

Joe knew the truth of all this, for he had learned the Indian customs.

"But, boys, yer place is back home with yer folks," he stated firmly. "The two horses rightfully belong to both of ye. They're fresh and ready to go I've got provisions in a couple of buffalo sacks that will feed ye fer a week. There's bright moonlight tonight. You boys git on yer horses and head east on the wagon trail. Keep goin' till ye git to Fort Laramie. The colonel in charge there may be able to help ye git to yer aunt and uncle you visited on the way West."

The thought of having a horse of his own appealed to Harry. He finally consented to leave. He didn't allow himself to doze off when the Indian family went to bed that night. As soon as he heard them breathing heavily, he wriggled quietly out of the tepee. The dogs all knew him and did not bark.

Ted and Joe had the horses all ready. Their food was in buffalo-hide bags tied together and thrown across each horse's withers. Ted had a stout strap tied to his rifle so that he could carry it on his back. They had no saddles but rode bareback, Indian fashion.

Joe gave them both a firm shake of the hand. Ted thought he saw a tear in the Mountain Man's eye as they rode off.

As soon as they were free of the camp, the boys put their horses into a gentle lope.

"Don't run 'em too fast," Joe had warned. "Keep 'em goin' along steady, except fer a rest every now an' then. Ye should be in Laramie by Wednesday."

Every four or five miles they rested the horses. Harry got
down on the ground and placed his ear to the earth.

"It's a trick the Indians taught me," he told Ted. "You
can hear horses' hoofbeats a long ways off if you listen carefully. There's no one following us so far."

They made a sharp turn in the road. There was a rustling
in the bushes behind them, and their horses snorted in fear.
Looking back, they saw a huge grizzly come out of a patch
of wild berries.

"Get your rifle! Shoot him!" yelled Harry.

But Ted made no such move.

"Joe always warned me never to bother a grizzly," he told Harry. "If you don't kill it with your first shot, you're in for trouble. And if I did kill it, we'd have to leave it here. Then any Indians following us would find it and could tell just how far ahead we were. Better not leave signs."

The horses were glad of this and galloped away from the scent of the bear as fast as they could.

At Fort Laramie the colonel remembered them.

"There's been many a wagon passing through here since yours. But none of them had twin boys like you. I've kept a daily record while I've been here. Let me look at it."

On his last year's record he found their parents' name and where they came from.

"Company G will be heading eastward next week," he told the boys. "You can ride along with it to Independence. Then you won't be far from your uncle's home."

The United States Cavalrymen were jolly with the boys. Ted and Harry enjoyed riding with them. Their captain put the boys at the head of the column.

They parted company at Independence, after the captain had found where their uncle and aunt lived and directed them to the road.

Their aunt was coming out of the henhouse as they rode into the barnyard and dismounted. They had grown so big that she did not know them. When they told her who they were, she threw her arms around them and took them into her comfortable kitchen to hear their story. She shed tears over the slaying of her sister- and brother-in-law.

When her husband came in from his plowing and heard their story he said, "Hang your things up right here, boys! We have no young'uns of our own, an' this quarter section I got from the gov'ment needs two strong boys like you to farm it. There's plenty of work for a trapper, too. Lot's of fur-bearin' animals are down near the creek."

Their aunt gave them chicken and dumplings for their dinner that day. Then each boy had two big pieces of her apple pie, with fresh milk from the cow to wash it down.

"It seems pretty good to have a real family again," Harry said.

"I'm glad we came East," said Ted, leaning back comfortably in his chair. "But someday I want to go back and be a real Mountain Man like Trapper Joe."